alcoholica
a love lay

Aditya Bhardwaj

BLUEROSE PUBLISHERS
India | U.K.

Copyright © Aditya Bhardwaj 2024

All rights reserved by author. No part of this publication may be reproduced, stored in a retrieval system or transmitted in any form or by any means, electronic, mechanical, photocopying, recording or otherwise, without the prior permission of the author. Although every precaution has been taken to verify the accuracy of the information contained herein, the publisher assumes no responsibility for any errors or omissions. No liability is assumed for damages that may result from the use of information contained within.

This is a work of fiction and does not resemble any events or person dead or alive.

BlueRose Publishers takes no responsibility for any damages, losses, or liabilities that may arise from the use or misuse of the information, products, or services provided in this publication.

For permissions requests or inquiries regarding this publication, please contact:

BLUEROSE PUBLISHERS
www.BlueRoseONE.com
info@bluerosepublishers.com
+91 8882 898 898
+4407342408967

ISBN: 978-93-5989-852-0

Cover Design: Sadhna Kumari
Typesetting: Pooja Sharma

First Edition: March 2024

To my mother

Usha

Without whose literary genes this could not have been accomplished.

Foreword

In these whirlwind times, when love has become more of a commodity rather than an emotion. The author brings you a fortifying tale of love which will leave you thrilled around every corner.

The love story is so enchanting it appears to be a cosmic intermingling of two immortals.

It breaks free the societal norms and discovers a new realm of love.

The captivating plot grasps you so firmly, that you encounter a climax at every step.

The phlegmatic approach of elaborating the fetters of the society and human mind is phenomenal.

Aditya has left no stone unturned to bring you a tour de force of the literary world.

Contents

The Encounter 1

The Cupid 8

The Escapade 14

The Agony 27

The Union 37

The Lament 44

The Salvation 52

About the Author 56

The Encounter

"Welcome aboard Sir!"

He was looking past the hostess who had just greeted him; past, at her companion. She looked reluctant in raising her eyes, avoiding his gaze. He paused for a while nodded then moved on towards his seat.

A new journey was to begin and fragrant memories of an old one just struck. A whirlpool of emotions arose in his mind. And what a journey it was. So lively, so fresh, so serene, divinely beautiful. A love chronicle.

Miracles, coincidences, and destiny reinstated their meaning once again in his mind. He had not had any encounter with the intriguing elements of nature for a long time now. So, it was indeed a pleasant surprise.

It was noon, and he already had had his morning quota of the nectar.

And what a plod it was! His long slender legs although not in rhythm due to the liquid gold still made such an effect on its audience as if a grandmaster was playing his masterpiece. Music in walk, walking music. Not dancing mind you. Dancing needs effort. It was the most effortless thing on earth.

Music in motion finally stopped as he approached his seat, stuffed his belongings in the overhead bin, and sat gently on his seat.

His eyes were so deadly and so alive. Deathless eyes. Eyes of a 5-year-old who is to discover the ocean of the world. Eyes so intensely hazel brown as if amassing the entire woods of a vast forest. Eyes that did not need words to express emotions. Eyes, deep and drowsy with alcohol.

Eyes that were still looking past everything towards the girl standing at the entrance of the aircraft, greeting guests. Eyes which had seen so much suddenly seemed to be vacant as if they had never desired to see anything else but her. As if the sole purpose of their existence was to see her. As if they would never be tired of looking at her, into her. Eyes that were watching the most beautiful creation of the Lord. They were fixed on her face. She knew it; as she had known years ago and she still did not know what to do, or where to hide, as she did not know then.

It was her deep desire to evaporate, to teleport to a place where only that pair of eyes would scrutinize her, where there would not be another soul, she still had that feeling after all these years.

Monotonous, vegetated life all of a sudden had a spark. She knew she could not be alive like this anywhere else, in anyone else's presence. Lifeless soul was once again ignited. Sparks could be seen on her face, she was blushing, confused. She wanted to shout and run away, go someplace and cry where no one could hear her. But she was a brave woman.

Oh! How could she have survived the tyranny of time, had she not been brave? She would have succumbed to whatever it was, if not love. And what was it? Hormones? Infatuation? Basic intense animal instinct? Love? Could there be something greater than love? This typhoon of emotions in human language is known as love, where everything is beyond control.

Emotions, intelligence, logic, sense of fear, nostalgia, everything, every possible human emotion is uncontrollable. It's love when everything is out of control. But what if it's in control and still you have never had this sensation before? Love at first sight? It doesn't invoke anger on the person you like. You don't ridicule him among your peers, you don't fear him, you don't want to snatch him away from this world, drag him to a place beyond existence and slap him. Slap him hard and then love him, love as no other woman has ever loved. What was it? Love? She did not know then, she did not know now.

It had been five years. She encountered love in these years a couple of times. She knew what love was. She gathered all her courage once again, and shouted in her mind, I don't love him! I can't!

She felt exhausted. She had to struggle so much whenever she had to command her conscience, her soul, her inner self of this and always felt drained as if she had spent all her energies, as if she had so strongly shouted to herself that her voice might reach heavens and the Gods might offer some help.

Help? What sort of help she sought? She asked herself. She did not need any help. She knew she did not love him. She had a good-going career and a smooth life. There is no place for him in her life, never was. She was a brave girl and everything was going to be fine, it was just a three-hour flight. She is doing her job. Everything will return to normal as soon as they land. Everything will be perfect as always. If she does not look into his eyes. That is a simple task, she just needs to avoid his eyes and that is it. So simple.

The simplest task was the hardest one. Not look into his eyes? Her religious side awakened. She knew she would need the help of God to achieve this.

He uplifted her from the dilemma as he had years back. She was as helpless then as she was today. He set her free once again. This was something that she had always hated. This magic spell that she could never break. This feeling of flowing as a river towards the sea, reluctantly. This feeling of being put on a swing, swerving gently, most gently towards the blue skies. To reach and pluck something no mortal has ever touched or felt. As if she is being dragged, dragged with her own will by a fine silk thread and if dragging is a brutal, bad, cowardly human gesture, she would call it 'divine' drag. Yes, that is what it was.

He was in command as always. This perturbed her more than anything else. It was as if she sought his permission to be free. This seemed to be appalling, senseless and incomprehensible after all these years.

He started to surf through his phone to give her space so that she could start moving around and the air-conditioned breeze carrying her scent would reach him. He could live that moment forever without complaining.

The plane started to taxi. He closed his eyes. He had a sense of deepest calm. He relaxed in his seat. He knew she had passed by. She felt like a zombie. Thanking him for his generosity to make it easier for her.

He was in a state of subconsciousness. Flashes started to appear. He was going farther and farther. Floating on a magic carpet. Oh God! Never stop this flight of the heavens.

A bolt of lightning struck him. The same pair of eyes that were so vainly and courageously trying to avoid his gaze were looking into him directly. A spell had been created. As if the energies were sharing their most beautiful, serenest, purest feelings through eyes. The collision seemed to be the best thing that could have happened to either of them.

"The entire package will cost you $ 999". He was explaining the deals to his US clients. She was bent just beside him trying to open the cabinet feveriously

"Would you be interested in tickets to Disneyland, Sir ?"He did not stop talking. His heart had. His eyes could not leave hers and vice versa.

He did not know what was he telling the client. She gathered the courage and asked "Could you help me with this?" He bent and opened the cabinet. Still talking over the phone, looking into her eyes.

He was so mesmerized, he did not realize when he opened the cabinet, and when she collected her belongings and moved towards her seat. His eyes were following her. It was like a time fissure. As if the earth had stopped rotating, the sun had stopped revolving.

She was already sitting opposite him. The mere plywood division between them did not seem to exist. She held his gaze. The entire universe was in sync with them. The moment was never to be lost. It had to be there in the history of time. This Fissure will capture these eyes clashing, heart pounding, five senses awakening to the fullest, forever.

They could not talk. No. It would spoil everything. Both of them wanted to live in this moment forever. Both wanted this to go on. It was as if the orchestra was playing their favourite song and they were submerged into the depths. There was thumping, thunders, clattering, hammering but it still seemed like music meant for relaxation, for sleeping, for meditation.

All the laws of nature were revoked. All the laws of the land were revoked. All mortal and immortal laws were to be tossed aside. They did not care if anyone was around. They did not care if their colleagues might be staring at them in awe. They did not care they might be doing something awkward, that did not belong to the place. They did not care if a bolt of lightning struck them, or the roof fell over or the entire hell broke loose. They did not care about anything except for looking into each other. They simply did not care. This was their first encounter.

This was when it all started. This was when began one of the most beautiful love stories of its time. Perhaps, a love story for the spectators. But for the two souls, it was a ruthless, crude, excruciating, divine, inexplicable life event.

Divine it was, for both of them did not understand what was happening. Both of them were clueless. They wondered if the almighty was as clueless as them. For in the time to come they were to discover, was this what had been defined as love for centuries? No, it was something beyond love.

Her friend jolted her, "Srisa, Srisa? What has happened to you? Did you see my headsets?"

"What? No. I have not". She replied finally. She smiled. This was a milestone, yes indeed. In the hustle and bustle and restlessness of twenty three years, today she felt as if she had finally reached a destination. This imparted some meaning to life. She was not sure what was coming ahead, but she felt like this must continue forever.

The Cupid

There was no way, they were to sleep that night. It was out of the question. They had been struck by the controversial Angel.

They were in the parking lot, from where the company's transport vehicles left. Their shifts were over. The pain was not. The Delhi sky appeared clearer. The stars were starrier. The breeze was cooler than the ice, it was a fine December night. The only thing missing was the fireworks. But they were crackling in their hearts and bodies.

His eyes followed her. Her eyes shyly captured the glances between chats with her friends.

They were to leave for two different locations. His heart was aching. Hers dancing.

Her cab approached. She boarded. She was not to look back. But she did. He was standing tall and straight. He was alone in the crowd. He appeared bewildered and composed. He meant what she was thinking about . He was looking straight at her.

After a sleepless night, on their way to the office, both of them were thinking about the day to come. There was joy, pain, misery, all at the same time. It was a simple job, talking to each other but it had been made complicated by destiny.

They both had friends, male and female. They laughed, partied, and cracked jokes together. But, here it was different. They knew they could not be friends.

The irony was, their workstations were facing each other. They were to look at each other but could not talk. Talking was out of the question, their hearts started pounding just at a mere glance.

Her shift started earlier than his. She held herself from looking at the entry door even at the slightest movement, but could not.

She wanted to make sure as soon as she caught a glimpse of him she would simply look down. Not looking at him was the key. The mind was firm. The heart was not. The heart was waiting, the heart was pounding. Pounding so hard as it would force its way out of the ribcage any moment.

She was sitting there lifeless and liveliest, simply waiting. She was stuck at the station. It had been more than twelve hours since she had last seen him. He was to be here now.

He was running late as usual. He was to report half an hour earlier. But he was a free soul. He was the wind. A windy storm. Restless and calm simultaneously. An enigma impossible to resist. A rage, a beast, a saint. Madness personified.

He entered. He saw straight into her. She was there for this look. A look of hunger. A look so wild, which depicted, how hard the last few hours had been without seeing her.

His steps were brisk and precise, making his way towards his workstation. Carefully and deliberately ignoring his managers, who had been eagerly waiting for him as he was again late today. A lady's voice shrieked, deliberately in a pitch higher so that it could reach the supervisors who were sitting in the next bay. "Kiesh! You are late again."

Kiesh. So that is him. She could not ask his name from anyone else. It would have been a blasphemy. If supreme almighty had planned this, he would take care of everything step by step, she was sure.

Kiesh. She said to herself. Her mind was filled with sheer pleasure. The name went through her brain like a symphony. *Kiesh.* Everything was so beautiful. Everything was going to be stupendous. She closed her eyes and rejoiced the Symphony of Kiesh.

"Kiesh! You are late again." Exclaimed the team leader. He kept walking and hurled her with the wave of his hand. All eyes were on him. For one, they were looking at one of God's best creations. Fair, tall, dark brown shoulder length hair, deep brown eyes, and a walk so firm and straight that could not be forgotten.

Dark blue linen shirt, light blue denims. And carved *kolhapuri chappals*. A *Chappal* yes, in the office. His attire betrayed the official dress code. As he betrayed all other official codes. One of which was substance abuse while on office premises.

This was the second reason everyone was glaring at him, men, women, everyone. And murmuring amongst themselves. They all knew he had been coming straight from the wine shop which was across the road from their office.

He took his seat deliberately ignoring Srisa. He had already looked at what he had to. He had freshly graduated from the training. So, the trainers were still on the floor to assist. He fetched his headsets, put them on and started his day. Srisa was on the other side, exactly opposite. Kiesh's trainer approached, sat next to him, and listened to his conversation with the client to make sure, he had got it all right during the training. Impeccable. The trainer thought in his mind. Kiesh was the best of the batch and only the trainer knew he had hardly attended any training sessions and he also knew where Kiesh had spent all his time of training. At the Delhi white Cappers, the retro bar across the road.

"You are sweating Kiesh." The trainer said. "Me? Kiesh replied in a husky, robust, bassy voice mellowed down by alcohol. "No, I am perspiring." Kiesh had chewed a few cardamoms to camouflage the smell. But still, the trainer could get an aura of vodka.

The poor trainer had no choice but to move on. He could not complain against Kiesh. No one could. He was an unproclaimed entertainer, no one wanted to lose. His presence had an energy, no one wanted to be deprived of. Everyone was en-circled with a sense of restlessness, eagerness, joyousness, stillness and liveliness. Who would want to get rid of an experience of so many colourful emotions, cumulatively?

Both of them were still looking at their respective screens. They did not have to look at each other any more. They could do without looking. They could smell each other, they could feel each other, they could sense each other. They were together all the time. They were now one and the same Kiesh and Srisa.

Almost everyone in the office had a love story. Someone was going around with someone. Some were engaged. Few had crushes, one-sided likings and cravings.

But still, they all were interested in Kiesh and Srisa. How would their story culminate? Wilderness and beauty. This was missing in their lives. An unruly alcoholic, raw and wild. And on the other side sophistication is at par. Excellence, grace and simplicity. There was something heroic about their meeting, which attracted everyone. This heroism was missing in theirs.

The show was on. There were many characters. But they all had been overshadowed upon his entry. The show had been overtaken by him. And now it was just his and hers. Kiesh's and Srisa's. They were all mere spectators now, who could comment, criticize, idolize, imitate, but they just simply could not be aloof, untouched, or indifferent to what they were witnessing.

They wanted to be the most sincere and honest audience, who would not want to miss even a single scene, lest it would spoil the entire script.

They were dumbfoundedly engrossed. The women especially, who had tried before to find a spot as his special one but in vain. They could not gather the courage to tame him. They were now curious to find out if Srisa was courageous enough.

The men on the other hand were jealous and angry at the same time. Jealous of him. And angry at her because they had all been turned down.

There was a certain enigma, a restlessness, and intrigue about the drama. Everyone was involved willingly or unwillingly.

The Escapade

The triggers had been set on both ends. Explosion was awaited. It was a test of time for both of them. The first move was expected from him. The women despite of all the women empowerment movements had been reduced to such a weakness that they would dare not attempt first. The women could crush the most lovable, uncontrollable, sweetest, harshest desire to dust. After years of training, women have developed that capacity. They have been trained by their aunts, society, friends, family and utmost by their mothers, that they must command men. They have developed that capacity very well but have lost a lot in the process.

It's not today nor yesterday, it's a practice of ages which has now penetrated deep into the bones through millenniums and centuries.

Command and rule men. And to do that the most effective weapon is their bodies, to which every man would succumb. They would rarely try to use anything else apart from their beauty and body. They would use kinds of things on their faces so that they glow. They would check their shapes and sizes constantly in mirrors. It's not their fault. They have been programmed since childhood. It's now become their religion. Their only religion is to control men. The only thing is when you try to control someone or something, you have already become weak. It becomes a mutual process when you try to control someone, you are also being controlled unknowingly. You cannot control someone without being controlled. And then it becomes mutual slavery. By the time women realize they have been practising the wrong religion, it's too late. Marriages fail, and live-ins are disrupted. Love has vanished.

It dawns upon them, it was all a pretext. His praising of my beauty, my intelligence, my honesty, and my innocence was all a pretext to capture my body. Once it's done life becomes lifeless. This eye- opening enlightenment is very difficult to digest in the early stages but then some have kids to raise, and some have bills to pay, so the lifeless life goes on. But it's painful and sorrowful.

They knew in the first place that it was a pretext but they would never dare utter the 'S' word. Their mind and souls have been trained like this. No. Camouflage it in the leaves of love, then it becomes sacred. The woman would never have the courage to say I want you. No matter if she is dying to sleep with the man. She would rather use all her skills, transferred to her by the wise ladies to make that man say' I love you'. No. Not I want you. I love you.

The tyranny of time. The tyranny of tutelage throughout the time.

The women themselves dig a pit so deep all their lives it becomes inescapable when they fall, fall in love because they have never been taught to rise in love. They must fall and take the man along with them. Then lead a life of toads in a well, who have an ocean of liveliness and energies to explore but they cannot because they have chained themselves. The man is chained to the body of the woman. He has nowhere to go. Nor does she. They enter the curse of marriage and ruin their lives and the lives of generations to come. They become the slaves of the society. And produce a generation of slaves.

Love is freedom, love is beyond any shackles, love is throbbing. Love is restlessness. Love is enchanting. Love is a neonate. Love is beyond the body. Love is, that the other person exists. They are there somewhere on this planet. The mere existence of the other person is sufficient for you to survive. But that is possible beyond marriage. Love is, that the other person exists and they think about you. That is love. That is motherly love. That is sisterly love. That is fatherly love. But when it comes to men and women, society interferes. The training of ages interferes. The future and security interfere. The inheritance of the kids, which are yet to be produced, interferes. Love takes a side stand. Love is lost slowly and gradually, forever.

So, love was the dilemma for Srisa. Her heart was revolting against the years-old training of her mind. She had to follow the contemporary rules. Make the guy say those three magical words first. He had to say it first. It's not a test of courage but the test of slavery.

Her ages-old training succumbed to her heart. But she had to keep her poise and stature. It was not just her after all. The centuries-old hard work and sacrifices of many women were at stake. She had to carry that flag high no matter if she had to put up a hard fight against her soul and heart.

Kiesh was aware of her dilemma. He had come across this before as well. He could see the desire dripping from her eyes. He could empathize with her helplessness. He knew all her courage would collapse against the shackles of society. He knew he had to make the first move. He knew it would spoil this aura, that was encompassing both of them. The serenity, the divinity, the awe, the tipsiness, the intoxication, all would be lost. But he would still do it. It was worth giving a chance. His desires and emotions had become so untamed and wild, that he had no other option.

He had come to the office late as usual that day too. He was supposed to report in at 9:00 PM but he came in at 11 p.m. He needed his 'me ' time at the bar across the road before reporting. He had been drinking all these years to bear the undue, unwanted vegetation that springs out during the rains. But now there was a beautiful bud amongst that vegetation. A beautiful pinkish, whitish bud that was gradually blooming into a flower with every passing day. The lifeless walls were swaying to welcome him as soon as he entered. The chairs were dancing. The monitor on his workstation winked and smiled as if saying 'Have you gotten your climax? 'Yes, he had. It was a climax indeed.

The only problem was there were hurdles at every step, as in any other true love story. Genuine love is always tested by time. And it rarely reaches its pinnacle.

He had come in late. His shift was to end at 6:00 in the morning. Hers at 5:00 in the morning. An hour earlier than his. He had come in late and had to leave early. He had to board her cab today. It had been almost a month. They were seeing each other every day. They were smelling each other through the air that carried the respective fragrances of their bodies. They were hearing each other 's voices, while they were talking to others. This was only fueling the desire burning in their hearts.

He was devising excuses to leave early that day. He knew it wouldn't be very difficult, as he had the skills to smooth talk his way out. It was 15 minutes to 5:00. He got up and made his way towards the manager's desk and declared "Boss I have acidity. Would go to the first aid room, get some medicine and would lie down for a while. The manager looked up at him and gave a smile while looking at his counterpart, who headed another team. He knew Kiesh could frame a white lie. He knew he had not come to seek his permission but just to inform him. He knew they could not stop the unstoppable. With a smile on his face, he said" Alright come on time tomorrow." Yeah sure. You know I'm rarely late" Kiesh replied. There was laughter in the bay once he left.

He hurriedly took the elevator and headed towards the medicine room which was across the road, the Delhi White Cappers.

He purchased a quarter of a bottle of whiskey and poured it into an emptied bottle of 500ml cola. It vanished within a couple of minutes as soon as it touched his lips. He was feeling better now. He headed towards the basement of the office building with firm steps.

It was already 5:00. The cabs had started lining up in the basement according to their destinations.

He quickly swayed his way amongst the crowd to the board where rosters were published. He checked the roster for Srisa's drop. Although his house was almost 40 kilometres away from hers. The cab would finish dropping off the employees in South Delhi itself. He had to manage to return to his place on his own. But it never crossed his mind. Such meagre things could not be a barrier against the events that were about to occur.

The cabs were all set to leave. He had spotted the vehicle's number from the roster. It was an SUV with seating for four in the last row. He rushed and opened the door to the cab. She was there, body without soul she was looking at him so closely for the first time. There was no barrier in between for the first time. She did not blink, did not smile. She did not know what to do because she was just a body without a soul. The soul had transgressed into a different dimension, a dimension that was beyond time.

Timeless entity where everything was progressing in slow motion. It was like a time-lapse. His moving slowly towards the cab, his hesitant pause before opening the door as if he would change his mind at the last moment and turn away. Her anxious heart missing a few beats went blank. Her heart did not know whether to beg someone for him to board that cab or to simply lock the door from inside so that he stays outside that cab and her life forever.

Her heart was as blank as her mind was. The heart had nowhere to seek refuge at that moment. She did not know whom she should beg and what to beg for. The heart was in a dilemma while the soul was enjoying the peace of timelessness. The beauty of slow motion. She wanted to live this moment again and again and again.

Kiesh opened the door and sat opposite her. It was vertical seating so they were facing each other now. There was a smile on his face. He greeted everyone with a smile, deliberately not being too much vocal and maintaining a distance, lest the smell of his freshly consumed liquid might be felt by his co-passengers.

She was sitting there in mere hollowness waiting for some sort of hint from him to react accordingly. He disappointed her. Their legs were almost brushing but he was cautious enough to make sure they did not collide. No, not now, not here. There is a time for everything. A particular portion of time was designed by the higher forces for the delightful ceremonies. A ceremony it had to be. But not now. They were both gauging each other. Talking was beyond question. A smile would spoil the moment. The restlessness in their hearts was subdued by the calmness on their faces.

He was there, this itself was like some sort of accomplishment, a victory. She was sitting there in front of him, so close that he could feel her breath on him, was an end to all his desires. The piety of that moment could not be exchanged with anything else. She's sitting there dumbfounded. He's slyly looking at her face once in a while. The wheels of the moving vehicle match the rhythm of their hearts. Some old classical songs playing on the stereo in the background.

What more could a human being dare to ask the Almighty? This was the essence of life. They both knew this moment would never happen again. The worldly physical desires would overpower their minds at a later stage but this event was pure bliss. This was beyond physical attraction. It was just two hearts beating, four eyes seeing each other, two ears alert to the slightest move of each other's shoes, two breaths, fighting each other, plunging in different directions and then making an effort to change their route, but merging into one as if their source was the same. Two breaths, divided by the bodies, united by the creator. Every sense was performing to the fullest as if they were delivering their best art on a stage show There was no room for mediocrity today. Their mouth was producing saliva at an astonishing rate. They were not anxious. It was pure harmony. It was, senses epitomized.

She jolted herself to the present, visual picture. He was there looking outside the window of the car, looking into dark eternity. He was there.

All other co-passengers from the rear seat had disembarked. It was just two of them now. They were not to talk. They were to live. The cab reached her house. She did not have the courage, but she did, she did smile and asked "Would you mind opening the door for me?" Melody to his ears his action was almost robotic, the door went ajar, he made way, she stepped down, and looked at him. There was that same roguish smile on his face and a cyclone in his eyes.

The next day was going to be a miracle. She had started to enjoy these sleepless nights. She could gaze at the stars all night thinking about him. She was so anxious as to what would happen next. He was not. Srisa was contemplating his next move while Kiesh was orchestrating the grand finale.

He was not anxious. He was not perturbed. He was calm as the sea before the storm. He was enjoying the journey. He knew the destination. But sometimes the journey itself is better than the destination. Not always, but sometimes. Those who say the journey is always better than the destination are fraudsters. Not always, but yes sometimes you want to live every moment on the way. It's not with a new path, it's with an unreturnable path. The journey of a lifetime, which will only happen once. Once you reach the harbour, you won't sail back. It's a one-way. You would never want to tread on it again. It's a once-in-a-lifetime affair. Once you have tasted bliss and ecstasy you would not settle for less. The journey is the pain, the terminus is the pleasure. Pain and pleasure.

Srisa woke up that morning after sleeping for just two hours. She had not slept, she had forcibly closed her eyes so that she could visualize her thoughts more vividly. With open eyes her thoughts about him were vibrational. With closed eyes they were sensational. Her mind wanted to sleep to continue enjoying the commotions but her body had become so outrageous and beyond the control of her conscious mind that it felt creepy. She doubted that she was undergoing some sort of mutation wherein her arms would sprout wings and she would fly straight away to him. The mutations were genuine and sincere. She was fathoming about how could bodily changes occur at the age of twenty-three. No, they could not. But alas! They should. They should.

How would she pass so many hours before she saw him again? Ten hours to her shift was like a decade. But she would want to wait for many such decades. This time-lapse was the magic. It made the moment of seeing him again so precious.

She was so exhausted by her bodily desires, she decided not to face him for a few days. She called in sick.

Kiesh did not look for her. He did not miss her. He was there on all three days on his seat as usual. He was at peace. He was calm. She was with him all the time. The cycle of time and seasons could not hold them now. Three days was not even a blink of an eye. Even three centuries would have been non-existential. He knew there would be a fourth day, a fourth century.

Srisa knew this was not the resolution. Not seeing him even aggravated the problem. The solution was nowhere in the realm of her conscious mind. The subconscious mind had entered an entirely new dimension which accumulated a variety of new feelings and emotions, that were so soothing and fulfilling, that reinstating to senses seemed like a sin. She was ready once again for the battle that was facing her. It was a long one she knew but there was no way of escaping it now. She was not sure about the outcome but it was a war worth living. The treachery of her soul was baffling. She was not prepared, her physical self had surrendered but her soul was so elated, it had taken the elevator to the utmost happiness. A sort of happiness that could not be disrupted by anything. It was a fresh experience for her, she was not sure what it was but it was something beyond her control. She entered the office. He was yet to come. She greeted her colleagues. Took her seat; and kicked off the system. And she started waiting for him. She could not help it. It was not a physical demand. It had become a spiritual obedience.

He came as usual. A little stagger indicated he had been missing her. Although it was not obvious nor visible to the naked eye, the stagger was felt by the naked heart. The stagger meant it was more than his routine drinking, the stagger meant he had been pumping himself to be stronger, and the stagger meant he had failed to do so.

He sat opposite her and started to wait for the dawn. The dawn that would bring him closer to her.

She was thrilled at the same thought. She had started to follow his wavelength. She knew he would follow her home again, today as well. She was ready for that sting and delight. The cabs were about to leave. She was looking for him. He came in like a gush of wind and sat so silently even the driver did not notice that another entity had entered the vehicle. It was winter. He opened the sliding window. The chill went through everyone present in the cab. But no one dared say a word of protest. He had been working for over a year in this office and made a reputation that no one would oppose him, including the driver. They all knew him via someone. The driver's via other drivers. The employees through other employees. So, there was no question of confronting him.

The chill of the December wind was felt by everyone. It was disturbing for the others while soothing for Kiesh and Srisa.

The ardour that had accumulated in their minds and bodies, blessed him for providing such a relief, even if temporary. It was pitch dark in the vehicle. One other female employee had deboarded a while ago. Both of them were exchanging glances without any expressions. The expressions were meaningless now. It was all imminent now what was to come. He had foreseen it. Srisa's latent mind had also. But her conscious, worldly limbic mind was revolting to save her dignity and feminist ego.

Although she knew her efforts were futile. His eyes were to be avoided and could not be avoided. The moment he looked at her, her soul surrendered. It experienced such joy and bliss that was inexplicable. The body kept its poise but the heart detached itself and started dancing to the rhythm of the wind. Her heart was pelting down with joy.

There was no stopping it. She dreaded the idea as to where this was heading.

This silent, beautiful, erotic pursuit carried on. But her sixth sense indicated, that so much pleasure could not go uninterrupted.

It had become almost a daily practice. Those couple of hours they spent together in the cab had become their entire life for the moment. The hearts were reciting poetry, the eyes catching glances once in a while. The mind was so calm and contained. The souls danced to every rhythm whether it was the jolts of the vehicle, the droplets pouring outside, or the wind playing with their hair.

The melodies of Kiesh and Srisa's hearts had environed the entire cab. Everyone was enjoying what was happening. The love in their hearts was so overwhelming, it seeped into everyone else around. The girls murmuring songs played on the stereo in the background. The boys who had earlier opposed Kiesh boarding their cab as it was not allocated to him, same boys joined the girls involuntarily. They were all singing and dancing in their places. No one cared if one was married, single, or dating. This was the juncture. This could not be lost. They were hands in hands, souls in souls, hearts in hearts. It was like a cosmic event and everyone around just got trawled into it. They had all become the purest form of love and enchantment. They had all become one. They were all Kiesh and Srisa.

The Agony

The tides far from the shore are a spectacle of beauty and calmness. The very same tides when monitored closely would be horrendous.

These very tides were being enjoyed by the entire office. It looked like a smooth-flowing infatuation, which was to turn into a full-fledged relationship eventually. But tides have their ways. Tides could not be tamed. The tides, when acquire their full form, play havoc everywhere.

The meeting of two tides rising in the form of Kiesh and Srisa, from opposite directions, were to collide for sure. The collision was going to be tremendous. But their journey towards each other was to destroy the path. It was an untreated path, unknown to almost everyone. Mixed emotions were prevailing over their intellect. One was attracting, one was premeditatedly repelling, unwittingly dying to greet the other side with open arms. The travel time between the meeting of two tides was agonizing. The destruction was inevitable.

Kiesh's cab expeditions went on and off. So became his daily routine to the office. He was missing from the office most of the time. She had no other option but to sit and think about him all day and part of night, until she fell asleep.

Srisa's ego once again jolted her. Knowing him she knew what he would be doing while he was away from the office. Drinking was just one part which did not bother her much. Her mind was flooded with other sorts of titillating thoughts. Would he be doing it with other girls? Whom? Why?

After a few days of this hide and seek and once she was on the verge of losing all her sanity, Srisa made a decision. She had to. Robin who had been trying to impress her so badly for the last few months. Robin was the key at the moment.

Robin felt like a baby ,who had been returned his favourite toy after a lot of fluttering of arms and legs when she allowed him to sit next to him and listen to his gibberish.

Kiesh came in the next day. The regular visits of Robin to her station could not go unnoticed. There was that iconic patent smile on his face.

Robin and Srisa going together for coffee and lunch breaks also did not go in vain. She did not have to check on him to see the impact. She knew it was going to create a stir if not damage him. She still felt too weak to deliver the kind of blow that would be hurting.

The calm in his eyes and the smicker on his face made her even more furious. She openly started flirting with Robin. Robin was in seventh heaven. Kiesh had probably traversed infinity. He seemed undismayed. Kiesh shook hands with Robin, talked to him as well, and went out with him to smoke as with all other colleagues. She knew Kiesh would not show emotion. Emotions were hard to come out of him. He was constantly in a state of bliss, untouched by worldly matters. He was always like that, content. But she knew she had managed to create turmoil in his heart. No matter how hard he appeared physically something was stinging inside. She could sense it. She felt victorious. She was happy.

The tidal collision that was around the corner was awaited to be spectated by everyone. The people were looking at Kiesh now with raised eyebrows. There were hushed burbles, that Kiesh might have given in or lost. Although everyone was doubtful about this. Kiesh did not have the image of a Casanova or a stud. These characteristics were somehow subdued. He never made any effort to portray himself like that. But there was this eerie sense about him especially amongst the females. The guys adored him because of his macho and outgoing personality. The females liked him because of the enigma. The feminine sixth sense always had this intuition, that there was more to his character than appeared to the naked eye. There was an experience awaiting. A splash of joy and happiness, and mildness that's always around him. But, they were to depend on him, if only he would allow them a dip in that ocean of unexplored pleasures.

Kiesh was casually friendly with everyone. But the girls wanted more. And as if God had listened to their prayers. A ray of hope appeared from the dark closed doors when they saw Srisa romancing with Robin. The efforts of Srisa to demean Kiesh, were turning otherwise and were creating different kinds of turmoils in hers as well as several other lives. The girls sensing a chance were all eager and started making flirtatious attempts.

Kiesh had never forgotten to thank the generosity of God. He had a natural attraction, which he never could comprehend. So he always thanked God. When you are the source of attraction you just need to pick. He always believed what belonged to him would be attracted to him.

And such a belonging came forward in the form of Lily. He found Lily sitting next to his workstation, as he entered the office. Lily had swapped seats with one of his friends.

The expression on Srisa's face was inexplicable. The rage in her eyes could be sensed all around. The air conditioning seemed to have failed with the vehemence of her vexation. She tried her best to suppress her emotions but it had become an involuntary function.

Kiesh and Lily greeted each other and he took his seat. He did not bother to look at Srisa. He knew.

The stratagem here became more interesting as Robin belonged to Kiesh's team, so he had to hop bays to reach .Srisa at whatever time he could steal by avoiding the managers. Break was a different story. They were out of sight somewhere. But Lily being in the same team had this arrangement sitting right next to Kiesh and right opposite Srisa, for nine hours. For nine endless hours!

It was unbearable. Srisa somehow managed the day and next day put in the request to change her workstation. But theirs, being a small process, did not have many options. So, she just managed to move a few workstations farther, but damn she was still facing them and going mad with fury.

Srisa could hear Lily giggling at Kiesh's jokes. What was she to do about her senses? Her senses? They appeared to be now performing at peak level. Every single word they were talking about was audible, every small action and touch, even if it was just a handshake, was viewed with hatred and disgust. What right did he have to touch her?

Srisa gathered her strength and tried to become as emotionless as she could be. She even tried to imitate similar things with Robin. She would giggle and get up with a swirl to go out with him during the breaks. Kiesh was unaffected. Because she didn't have to look at him. He did not have to look at her.

Kiesh would enter the office premises in his usual manner. Calm and composed. A hint of alcohol was always there. The lights of his Bay were to be switched off, as instructed by him. Some close friends who sat near the switchboards took care of this. He would greet his peers. And then greet Lily. That was the blow. Now she had taken a special place. She was not the first to be greeted, but the last. Srisa called for all the strength from the divine feminine. It's not her now but her amour propre at stake. How could such a joyous, loveable and amicable-looking creature be so callous?

Kiesh was singing, looking at Lily "Your eyes that emit this pinkish yearn, make my heart feel drunk."Srisa listened furtively. He did not even slightly look at her. He did not have to. His full attention was on Lily.

These harrowing events went on for a couple of weeks.

And then one perishing day Kiesh came, sat beside Lily. Lights were switched off as instructed and they started talking. Srisa overheard and grasped some words like pictures and then came the blow. She heard the word nymphomaniac. That is it. She made out where this all was heading. Or what could have already happened?

The Princess' peace was broken. She summoned Robin to her station. Srisa whispered something in Robin's ear and then he hurriedly rushed towards the manager's desk to seek permission to leave an hour earlier than the specific time. Everyone was having fun including the managers. He was permitted to leave early.

Srisa got up, looked at Kiesh with a smirtle, shut down her system and began to leave with a swirl. Her lush brown, waist-length hair was facing Kiesh. Robin followed impatiently. Kiesh kept busy with his work. Lily was looking at him. Almost everyone was. The drama was taking a new turn. Everyone was thrilled except for Kiesh. Kiesh was silent. The silence was somewhat unbearable. The silence of a dormant volcano, which could erupt anytime, lest it's better to maintain a healthy distance. Lily did not dare talk to him, since the departure of Srisa and Robin.

Kiesh finished his work, waved his goodbyes and left as on any other day. As soon as he came out, he called Robin. Robin did not dare to.not answer his phone. Kiesh had always been amicable and helped him on a few occasions. Robin remembered the day, he met with an accident and how he got surrounded by the locals as a girl got injured in the mishap. It was Kiesh who had come to his rescue mid-shift.

"Where are you? "Kiesh asked. There was a hesitant pause on the other end and then Robin replied " Why?" I asked, where are you?" Kiesh repeated. Robin just uttered out of confusion and gratitude I am at the Devil's Disco. Kiesh knew in which hotel the Devil's Disco was. Kiesh disconnected and called another friend Joy and they headed straight towards the Devil's Discotheque.

Srisa had somehow collected her strength to take Kiesh off her mind. She did not care whether that was out of grudge or disgust or both. Robin and Srisa were dancing. They both inherited brawn from each other. Robin suddenly wrapped his hand around her waist. She did not resist. Yes, she told herself she could endure this. It was a gesture, to pull away from the crowd to a more cosy and silent place. Srisa obediently cooperated. Srisa guessed Robin wanted to take her to the parking lot where his car was parked. They started moving towards the exit gate, hand in hand trying to smile at each other.

Robin pushed the door with one hand and there he was. The Deity himself trying to explain something to the bouncers in his charming voice. One of the bouncers politely nodded," Sir, please try to understand, the policies are policies and they apply to everyone even if you are a regular guest. We cannot allow you to enter inside in these slippers."

Srisa was dumbfounded. She did not know, whether, she was more shocked or humiliated. Her conscious mind heard the words slippers and her eyes moved to Kiesh's feet. His overt kolhapuri chappal, which he would often wear to the office, even after several warnings by the management. The Deity had reached the Devils. Kiesh seemed no longer interested in haggling with the disc staff. His task was done. Robin was looking ineptly here and there, somewhere in space deliberately avoiding Srisa's probing eyes.

Srisa knew all her plans had to be dumped. Her desires were killed and aroused. The comparison was standing right in front of her. The Deity had reached the Devil's. Robin shook hands with Kiesh quickly and hurriedly followed Srisa who had already left without saying a word to anyone. She did not speak a word with Robin on her way back Home.

Reaching home she slammed on the bed, face down. Being furious and agitated won't suffice her feelings and emotions at that moment. Another defeat at his hands. Who was he, after all? Who was he?

The next few days in the office were deadly. Robin's visits to Srisa's desk were forbidden. Kiesh also did not want to add insult to injury, so he maintained a safe distance from Lily.

After a few days, when their affliction became too unpleasant, Kiesh decided to break the ice. He was with friends and colleagues at the Delhi white cappers and had had more than a few drinks. He was always joyous and cracking jokes which betrayed the storm that was raging in his heart. He was waiting for Srisa's shift to get over.

He entered the parking bay not staggering. He never staggered, but he did look exhausted today. The turmoil in his mind which had been hovering for the past few days, was tiring. He searched for her cab. He spotted the cab and she spotted him. Her disgust towards him had not diminished even an ounce since that hapless day. It was almost a hundred meters distance between them. He started walking towards the cab when a short heightened man with broad shoulders intervened in his manoeuvre. Kiesh's adventures were quite famous in the office. Srisa could not figure out, why that man had crossed Kiesh's path, but the conversation between them seemed ere long heated. The cabs had already started to move. She was the last one in the back seat and she had still not closed the door. Her heart arbitrarily waited for him. Three more men approached Kiesh and the short man. Holy lord! She exclaimed in her mind. It's the Admin. Her heart sank and started racing. Caught drunk on office premises was a straight termination. Zero tolerance. The driver came and banged the door. Their cab pushed forward, her eyes fixed on Kiesh and the administration staff. She had a last vision of Kiesh wrapping his hand around the short guy's shoulder and taking him aside. She started hating herself at that moment. She blamed herself as she had been cursing him badly and thoroughly for the past many days. Oh God! She felt brain fogged and dizzy. She never meant this. This was the last thing she wanted to happen on earth.

Recognizing Kiesh's character she knew if he was terminated, it would end everything. She had tears in her eyes, her throat aching. Would he be gone forever?

The Union

It was a night of trial for Srisa. Sleep was miles away. Vicious thoughts had captured her mind. She was so sorrowful, that it was sort of a new feeling for her. She had never been so upset in her life before. She solely blamed herself for all the ill thoughts she had been contemplating for Kiesh, for the past couple of months. She was in a state of hysteria thinking that the seat opposite her in the office would now be vacant.

She was so distressed, that she hardly slept the whole night. The next day she woke up with a heavy head. Last night's events hovering in her mind. Her brains were being hammered. She had no desire to go to the office. But she had to. She had to check the power of her prayers. She had to go and check herself. She could not leave him alone at this crucial point. She could not withdraw now. It was too late. She must go and face the squall.

Srisa opened the door to the floor and there he was talking candidly to Joy. Her legs were shaking. She gathered her strength and moved towards her seat. She took her seat with a sigh of relief. Closed her eyes and thanked the Almighty. And then she overheard the conversation between Kiesh and Joy. Joy asked him curiously "And then, what happened next?" Kiesh replied in his custom valiant tone "What happened next?," I took the admin guy aside and showed him this". Kiesh was wearing a green leather jacket, he slightly opened it so that Joy could get a glimpse of what was inside. Joy's mouth was wide open, "you showed him this?" Kiesh put a finger on Joy's open mouth and completed his sentence "Chocolates. I offered him chocolates as a bribe." Srisa knew this was far from the truth.

She later learnt from her sources that it was a pistol, he used to carry. A pistol in the office? The rascal would always remain a rascal. All her pity and guilt vanished. Look at that face and his deeds! So unpredictable. Her heart again pondered her, why did she fall for him in the first place? Why is she still so attracted to him? She laughed to herself. Her soul repelled him and her heart charmed. She smiled again. The days were passing by but she was moderate now because Lily had started going around with another manager, Irfan, and distanced herself from Kiesh

Srisa had been noticing for the past few days that Kiesh was sitting idle and just gossiping with one or the other compeer. She got to know the reason the day when one of the managers came howling like a wolf, " Kiesh why? What happened?" Kiesh replied slowly and amicably," The headset boss. There ain't any headsets. "The manager turned to the supervisor and growled," Where have the headsets gone?". Supervisor sheepishly replied," Sir I count them always and there is one or two missing every day". "Check the cameras now" The manager ordered

The cameras were not to do anything. Everyone knew on whose instructions the headsets were concealed. And they also knew how skilled the Deity and his disciples were. Srisa murmured to herself, rascal would always remain a rascal. Kiesh and Srisa's affection got a new spark. The ice was broken after that unfateful event in the parking lot. They were both their real self again. The burden of pretentious lovers had been shed from their shoulders. They both slyly caught each other's glance now and then. The beauty in everything got reinfused. The office floor which had started giving the vibes of a hospital, was again alive with smiles and laughter.

Kiesh entered his bay with a pet cold drink bottle in his hand. He sat beside Ramya and offered her the bottle. She took a sip and made an unpleasant face while replacing the cap. Srisa could comprehend what was inside the bottle. So, it was not just his charming looks that cheered the girls, free service of alcohol was another reason. That one sip was no less than ambrosia after quibbling with clients over the phone. Srisa again questioned herself, who was he? Would you ever come across another personality, so dark and so vibrant? But Srisa was taut. She knew what she and Kiesh shared could never be meddled with.

The days rolled by. Srisa's and Kiesh's initial penchant and desolation became stronger and stronger. She sometimes wondered what is he waiting for now. and wondered if there were some special institutions one must attend to understand characters like Kiesh. But she waited.

It was like any other day. Kiesh came in and positioned himself adjacent to Joy. Joy was not feeling well. So he was sitting head down on his desk. Kiesh asked," Hey what happened? "Joy replied "Headache." Usually, you ought to use the sick room if you are not feeling well. So that it does not affect the productivity of rest of the staff. But it was Kiesh's Bay after all. It ran by his rules.

The floor appeared a bit rackety today. The call flow was on the higher side as compared to other days. The managers and supervisors were on their feet. A supervisor named Yuvraj came rushing to Kiesh's Bay and shouted," Wrap up your calls guys". His vision fell on Joy, and he yowled" Hey, what happened to him?" Kiesh was the first one to reply "He is not feeling well. He's on his period. The girls from the other team were shocked. The girls from Kiesh's team covered their mouths with their hands. The supervisor turned into an effigy for a while. And then there was a riot of laughter. The supervisor looked straight at Kiesh and said" gang of goons" and left the bay with a stomp. Gang of goons, yes that's what he had transformed everyone into. The most joyous goons that had ever lived on this planet.

Kiesh had returned to his old charming self and his cheap sense of humour made everyone laugh. It was his tits and bits of taunts that would bring a smile to everyone's face. One of the managers was coming out of the conference room after a meeting with a female American client and Kiesh would sneer at him "Hey boss you look extraordinarily happy today, what's the matter ?"The manager burst out in laughter including everyone else present there.

Robin was trying to dissociate himself from Kiesh after that night at the discotheque. But one unlucky day Kiesh caught hold of him when a seat next to Robin was vacant. They exchanged greetings and went back to their work. Mid work while both of them were wrapping their calls with notes, Kiesh suddenly announced looking at Robin "Hey guys "Everyone paid attention" I am throwing a party. A group sex party and everyone has to bring his girlfriend along." There were whispers and slight chuckling in the Bay. Robin's face was pale. He still managed to smile. Srisa who had been conditioned by now to never miss a word that came out of Kiesh's mouth, immediately and involuntarily got up and came next to Robin. She leaned over Robin's desk and while looking at Kiesh said" I'm not your girlfriend Robin. Am I?" Kiesh caught a glimpse of her milky white cleavage when she leaned. His mind got such a kick that tens of thousands of litres of alcohol couldn't ever give. It all looked mechanized. She got up, went there and returned to her seat. It took her a few minutes to realize what had she just done.

It was now Kiesh's turn to go sleepless. Her face, her green eyes, her lips like rose petals. She looked like beauty epitomized.

Her eyes had the same iota that he saw on the first day of their rendezvous. The same mischief. The same desire and longing.

The next day kiesh came up with the resolution. The lights of his bay were switched off as he entered. He slowly and casually sorted out his things. She was sitting there already. A few minutes after settling down, he stood up looked straight at Srisa and started singing, " Oh innocent! you agree, or my life would turn into debris."

Srisa felt like someone was caressing her body with a thousand flowers. Her heart beating rapidly. She got up and left the floor with a smile on her face.

Srisa left the office premises. It was raining outside. She wanted to get drenched. But it was mid-shift. Who cares about the shift, the office, or the world anymore? She felt like her chained soul had been freed after centuries. Her feet felt so light as if they were an inch above the ground and she was skating in the air. She stepped into the rain. Every falling droplet, touching her body felt like a blessing from the Elysium. A reward for the courage, she had shown and stood the test of time. She was gloomy and ecstatic.

Srisa jolted herself to her senses and realized she was still left with a few hours, to be spent in the office. Her mind was thoughtless, her actions were motorized, and she just had an image in her mind of a man with long hair, singing songs for her.

On her way back to the office floor, Srisa chose to take the stairs instead of the lift. She wanted to spend some more time with herself. Their office was on the fifth floor. She started climbing the stairs swaying a bit and singing in her mind "Oh innocent, you agree, or my life would turn into debris". She didn't realize when she reached the fifth floor. He was standing there all alone smoking. She looked at him, then shyly made her way to open the door of the fire exit. He grabbed her by the hand. She felt as if the lightning that was thundering outside just struck her with full might. He pulled her towards the stairs with a jerk.

She started moving upwards facing him. Their eyes fixed on each other. After a few minutes, which felt like an eternity they had reached the topmost floor. It seemed like a miracle, but not a single person was present in the entire staircase that day.

Kiesh and Srisa. All alone in the whole universe. The walls, the stairs, everything else had just disappeared. Kiesh's hands moved so swiftly, that all the buttons of her satin shirt plummeted like seasoned leaves in the autumn. He was skilled as a magician. Within minutes both of them were de-clothed. Her hands, instinctively, covered her feminity. Her breasts were trembling, with cold and excitement, like a pair of white doves gossiping with each other.

He was jubilating while looking at the marble statue, that had been vitalized. He came a step closer. His one hand moved around her waist, the other supporting the back of her head. He kissed her so hard, she felt like her lips would bleed. Mouth on the mouth, legs on legs, soul on soul. His legs felt like hot metal cutting through ice. The union materialized into an amalgamation of pleasure and pain.

The Lament

Srisa called in sick the next day. She was still postulating the previous day's events. Her body seemed as if it did not belong to her anymore. She was just a soul now. A soul free to fly anywhere but it was attached to invisible strings being held by someone else now. And she wanted this bond to last for a lifetime. She would think of his hands, his lips, his face and smile to herself.

Her mother kept coming into her room to inquire if she was well because she had not eaten anything the whole day. Srisa could not explain to her that her hunger had been gratified by something more delicious and placid. She kept waking up with his caresses and going back to sleep again for repetition of the same.

She hardly ate anything for the next three days. She felt so suffused. She was still trying to contemplate whether what she had done was correct. Her soul was free but her body was still chained to the societal norms. But, what had she done? It was he, who had done that to her. She knew how badly she would fail if she ever tried to express this misconduct to anyone. She would not be able to convince even herself. She was in such a dilemma as to what to do next. She had slept with a man to whom she had never spoken a word with? Who would believe her? That was one thing she was never going to disclose to anyone. She would never spoil that avowal. But, her traditional conscience was vexing her. She made love to a man, she had never spoken with? The only words they shared, were the sounds of pleasure.

This was a paradox that she had to solve herself. Srisa was visiting the office after a three-day sick leave. She was still in a different dimension. Dimension of love. She was buried in her thoughts. He was missing from the floor. She thought he might have taken a day off. But when she did not get to see him for another three days, she enquired a friend, who confirmed he had gone on examination leave for one month. "What?" She exclaimed and then fell silent. Wait a minute. He had gone on examination leave? It was outrageous. She felt betrayed and humiliated. The imp had such an audacity to not even say a single word or leave a message through a friend after what all happened between them. Disgusting. She knew he had her phone number and she also knew that he would never call.

Srisa spent a few days in the office contemplating what to do next. The boys were keen to know if they had a second chance. After all they did not abort their procreation. Robin made another attempt. Srisa also tried to contribute but it was all ineffectual. She was frustrated after a few days

The problem was now she knew what it was. She had experienced it first-hand. It refuted all the theories of love that she had heard and practised before. This was different. It was disturbing, it was aching, it was delicious, it was not that, but it was the best. She could not have settled for anything less now in life. She did not want to. And yet it was so frightening.

Aloofness from the world, liking just one person so much, why? She was chained and she was free. She was humiliated and she was enjoying it. Her ego was hurt and she wanted it to be shattered. She had become the most egoist and most egoless woman at the same time.

She was free as she had never been. She could achieve anything in the world at present. She was so powerful and so powerless. She had touched the highest. She had touched the best.

She knew the difference now. That was the problem.

Srisa was so badly disheartened and abashed that she decided to take revenge. A revenge that matches the intensity of the flagrant act that he had committed. She pondered over the same, and being a woman of character she made up her mind. She knew what she had decided was devastating for both of them. But she was ready to bear the collateral damage. She was so furious.

The next day she went straight to her manager's desk and declared she would like to put down the papers. The manager tried to retrieve her by explaining how she could be promoted next year and had a bright future with the organization. But she was firm. Her exit from the office was with a smile on her face and a wound in her heart.

Kiesh returned after his month-long ostensible examination leave. Everyone awaited his reaction, but there was none. He kept coming to the office regularly. He was as jovial as always. After almost a week, Joy informed him what had happened. Kiesh's face was expressionless. He was silent for a minute and then laughed out loud "This is the cycle of life my friend. One exits another enters". Joy could feel the pain in his words.

Kiesh, while on lunch breaks had seen some of Srisa's enthusiasts surfing through her social media. He saw some of her pictures in a red uniform. He could make out it belonged to some airline. His oculars were later confirmed by Joy that she had indeed joined the aviation industry as a cabin crew.

Lily again started sitting next to Kiesh, before some other girl did. She tried to cast her old charm but Kiesh always seemed lost. He was lost before as well. But this time it was different. They were talking. They were laughing together at his silly jokes. But Lily could sense it was not the old Kiesh, she had met the first time. She inferred something had shuffled off this mortal coil.

This reconciliation of Kiesh and Lily seemed very irksome to Irfan, who was Lily's self-proclaimed boyfriend. He was a supervisor ,so Lily had made friends with him to avail the perks like coming late some days and logging off early. But Irfan had developed a raw nerve for Lily and he was very upset with Kiesh and Lily's kinship. Irfan was just looking for a chance to settle scores with Kiesh.

It was public that Kiesh was drunk every day. His drinking had now been acknowledged more widely because he had been drinking heavily after Srisa's departure from the office.

"This is your day,"Irfan told himself. He approached Kiesh and Lily and ordered him "Kiesh, you won't be sitting here tomorrow onwards." He meant next to Lily". Your workstation has been changed." Kiesh paused for a while and with raised eyebrows asked in his intoxicated voice "may I ask who changed it? I will sit where I please. This company does not belong to anyone's father". This was it. This was what Irfan had been waiting for. He headed straight towards the human resource team, to inform them about Kiesh's muddle. Lily rushed after him and pleaded with him not to do so. She somehow managed to persuade him.

Lily returned to her seat." What is your problem Kiesh"? And she gave him a small hug. Kiesh knew that she had been trying to fill up the void that was created by Srisa. Kiesh replied in his firm voice," The problem is not just with me. The problem with almost all of us is , we keep creating superficial bridges all our lives. I believe in crossing the bridge when we will come to it. Why to cross a bridge which is not there? Why to create unnecessary obstacles throughout life? Why? There is no problem in anyone's life, it's ecstatic. It's beautiful. It's serene. Self-fulfilling. We create bridges of schools, colleges, money, cars, houses."

He continued " This permeates so deep down into our subconscious mind that we can not sit idle. There's restlessness. we would not sit idle for a while and enjoy the beauty of the sea, flowers, bees, and trees. Everything is divine. Everything is pure. But we take it for granted. We wait. There's time to do this later. No! this is the time. All the years, you kept skipping what you want to do the most. You wanted peace. Where's peace these days anyway? Peace has become synonymous with death and the death we are living every day has become synonymous with life."

Kiesh paused for a while and resumed "You have a house, and you have money already but you have to become a CEO, you will create a bridge. You have a car, you want a bigger one. You will create a bridge. There's no hunger, you will create hunger. There's no thirst you still need a cola. There's no anger, you want to be angry. There is no love. You will create it. That's where the problem starts. If you have to create love, it's cosmetic. It will never give you contentment. Nature is so fulfilling. So spontaneous. It creates everything .You are here to enjoy in harmony. But we keep fighting it all our lives. We betray nature. We blaspheme against it. We fight it. And we lose in the end What a waste!"

Lily got her answer. She now knew, what she was trying to do was inefficacious.

The next day, Kiesh's manager, Yusuf came to his seat and summoned him inside the conference room. Both of them shared an affable relationship. Yusuf began with a heaviness in his voice" Why are you doing this to yourself?" Kiesh"s face was blank and he asked, "What am I doing to myself?"

Yusuf pulled his chair closer to Kiesh, "Listen. I won't ask why you have been drinking so much lately. It's quite evident. But I must ask you, not as a boss but as a brother why don't you join some other organization? You would get a better salary."

Why don't join some other organization? How could Kiesh ever tell him that he had been tethered to this place? He still sees Srisa's silhouette sitting in her seat, and still smells her redolence in the air But he was generous enough to reply with "How could I join some other organization, I like this company. He replied with a smile on his face. Yusuf got up "Alright then. Do as you please. But you must remember I am not the only manager on this floor. There are others, who are not very much happy with your behaviour." Kiesh again smiled and replied," I understand and I am obliged". They both looked at each other and Yusuf left the room.

Kiesh could perceive that his days were numbered in this facility. He was going to get the axe anytime now. But he had decided to leave as a martyr rather than a deserter.

All the supervisors and a few managers had lobbied against Kiesh. They were just waiting for the right opportunity. The HR manager had been deliberately requested for the last few days to be present during the night shift.

One day Kiesh was sitting in his seat inebriated and singing songs, "You consider or not, I have considered you my God", when one of the supervisors asked him to approach the HR room.

Kiesh stood up elegantly. Shut down his system. Put down his handset in its place. Used a mouth spray to ward off any unpleasant smell and approached the HR room.

The human resource manager was saying "Do I need to tell you why you have been summoned? " Kiesh replied with a grin," No."

The manager said in a resolute tone," You must leave Kiesh"

Kiesh again smiled, said thank you and left.

While exiting the office building a few colleagues asked" Hey Kiesh, where are you going?" He replied in his custom valiant flair" Delhi White Cappers". They all laughed. He did not tell anyone about what had just happened. So, that was how Kiesh bid farewell to the company where he had spent the most wonderful moments and a thaumaturgic night of his life. He left the company, where he had lived an absolute aeon, with a twinkle on his face.

The Salvation

Kiesh was not heartbroken nor was he shattered. He had touched the Valhalla. He did not miss Srisa. She was always there with him. Bodily and worldly pleasures are afar gratification What they shared between them was a consortium of souls.

Both of them had reached the pinnacle of proclivity. Even Srisa could not deny that. They knew they had had the best that love could offer, and they would live with it forever.

A person is malcontent when he is involved in bodily cravings. Their lovemaking was celestial. Srisa was hurt indeed and did not know how to react at his preposterous behavior, so she decided to maim him too.

Although she knew very well that it would be in vain. This was what perplexed her even more. The sort of credence that he radiated did not belong to this world. He was always so sure of himself and his actions, as tranquil as a dense forest. This had perturbed her even more. Kiesh was like a gently flowing river whose depth was bottomless and whose periphery, no one had ever seen. He was infinite blitheness in the flesh.

Kiesh spent a couple of years doing odd jobs. He had never been stable anyway, at any of his jobs. The only immutability he found was, in the company, of Srisa. He kept moving from place to place but he was never despondent. His inner self was still making efforts while hopping places and flights to see Srisa once again. He started frequent air travel in the belief that he would come across the entity that had afforded him enduring tranquillity.

Joy called him one day asking about his current orientation. Joy wanted to know if Kiesh had turned the corner after his desolation. Kiesh replied in his wonted intrepid way" My dear Joy? Why have you become so morose? At least do some justice to your name."

He pursued, " You know what, sadness and happiness are synonymous. It is the same for me. I did not practice it. But it has been like that always for me. It's not something I appreciate, it's a rather seriously risky thing. But it's ecstatic. You start finding joy in grief. You are never sad then. Medical experts would describe it as some sort of disorder, I'm sure. But affliction and rapture become one. Then you can't distinguish between the two. It's beautiful, it's awful, it's madness, it's divine.

"After all, what is suffering without delectation and delectation without suffering? They will both lose their significance in the absence of another. For me, it has always been coalescence of both. After being in such a state for a few years there's no pain. Pain becomes a pleasure. It's absurd but it's true. It's attachment and detachment at the same time. It's like enjoying your sickness. Sickness and health become one. To achieve this you have to rise a little bit higher, not too much, just a little bit above others. Too much will detach you completely. It's such a waste not to enjoy this beautiful body, His beautiful creations. Rising above a little bit gives you a clear vision of the real purpose of this life. Then you see this world from a different perspective. You are a part of it and you are partying. Partying hard."

Joy could not perceive any dejection in Kiesh's dialect but he could sense, that Kiesh had transformed into a runnel which was headed towards merging with the prodigious ocean.

And after almost five years, which seemed like five decades, of excruciating interlude, Kiesh was here today on the flight, which was being apportioned by his inamorata.

Both of them should have been uncomfortable. But they felt composed after forever and a day.

Srisa and her colleagues were doing their quotidian drill. She came to Kiesh's seat and asked his fellow passengers, not looking at him "Would you like to have something else, Sir? " "Did you miss me?" Kiesh said abruptly. She was angry, her legs quivering, she collected her strength, gathered herself and asked escaping his eyes "Would you like to have anything else, Sir? " A last drink please ." Kiesh enjoined.

Srisa hurried herself towards the kitchenette, quite not completely comprehending his words. She knew he had at least four drinks before this one. But she had no courage left. Why was she doing this to herself? She was frustrated with the thrill and asked her colleague to serve him.

Srisa's colleagues did find her behaviour anomalous but they could not gauge the reason instigating it.

Her colleague shrugged, poured a drink and approached Kiesh's seat. Suddenly there was a rumpus and commotion. Srisa straight away looked towards Kiesh's seat. No, it was not because of the turbulence of the aeroplane.

Srisa's colleague was shaking Kiesh "Sir, can you hear me? "Kiesh was still as a cadaver.

Srisa was no longer in that aeroplane. She skipped through time to the day, when they both had sighted each other for the first time. She said to herself bravely No! No!

She was standing very still, still as if all life had been vacuumed out of her. Still, fearing the whole world would collapse if she moved an inch. Her eyes were looking straight into his.

There was a doctor present on the flight who was trying to resuscitate Kiesh. After a while, the doctor declared" Sorry, he is not breathing".

"He is not breathing," Srisa said to herself. Oh, so now he's not breathing. She laughed to some degree. How would she ever tell the world that, he was the breath himself? How could the breath not breathe?

The doctor with the assistance of the crew deposited Kiesh back into his seat.

Kiesh's eyes were open and pacific. The eyes of a pietist who had attained redemption. His face had the homogeneous accustomed lucency and glitter.

Srisa looked into those hazel brown eyes and then she fell down,tears fleeing her eyes as if they would never stop. Tears that seemed to flood the entire aircraft and drown the creation. And then she screamed! Kiesh!!!

He was still looking into her.

About the Author

Aditya lives in Delhi. He has worked in Delhi ,for almost ten years, as a voice coach.

He spent few years in Dubai working as a Travel consultant.

This is his first book.

www.ingramcontent.com/pod-product-compliance
Lightning Source LLC
LaVergne TN
LVHW061345080526
838199LV00094B/7379